# Max and

## and
## Zoe

The Science Fair

by Shelley Swanson Sateren

illustrated by Mary Sullivan

PICTURE WINDOW BOOKS
a capstone imprint

Max and Zoe is published by Picture Window Books
A Capstone Imprint
1710 Roe Crest Drive
North Mankato, Minnesota 56003
www.capstonepub.com

Library of Congress Cataloging-in-Publication Data
Sateren, Shelley Swanson.
  Max and Zoe : the science fair / by Shelley Swanson Sateren ; illustrated by Mary Sullivan.
      p. cm. -- (Max and Zoe)
Summary: Searching for a really cool science project, Max decides to demonstrate how dogs can read faces, with Zoe's help.
  ISBN 978-1-4048-7202-8 (library binding)
  ISBN 978-1-4795-2330-6 (paperback)
1. Dogs--Juvenile fiction. 2. Human-animal communication--Juvenile fiction. 3. Science projects--Juvenile fiction. 4. Helping behavior--Juvenile fiction. 5. Elementary schools--Juvenile fiction. 6. Best friends--Juvenile fiction. [1. Dogs--Fiction. 2. Human-animal communication--Fiction. 3. Science projects--Fiction. 4. Helpfulness--Fiction. 5. Elementary schools--Fiction. 6. Schools--Fiction. 7. Best friends--Fiction. 8. Friendship--Fiction.]
I. Sullivan, Mary, 1958- ill. II. Title. III. Title: Science fair.
IV. Series: Sateren, Shelley Swanson. Max and Zoe.
PZ7.S249155Mdt 2013
813.54--dc23

                    2012047382

Designer: Kristi Carlson
Printed in China by Nordica.
0413/CA21300452
032013      007226NORDF13

# Table of Contents

Max and Zoe met at the library.

"Try this book next," she said.

Max studied the book with the science experiments.

"Nothing fun in this book, either," he said.

"Our science fair topics are due tomorrow," Zoe said.

"These are all so boring," said Max.

"Just pick one," Zoe said. "It doesn't have to be perfect!"

"But I want my experiment to be the best," said Max.

"Okay. Good luck!" said Zoe as she grabbed her books and left.

Max was frustrated. He didn't want to pick a boring project.

Max went home and searched

for more ideas.

"All boring," he groaned.

"You have to pick something,

Max," his mom said.

Max frowned and went to his
room.

Buddy curled up on his lap.

Max gave Buddy a big hug.

"You understand me, don't you, Buddy?" asked Max.

"Woof!" said Buddy.

Max thought for a minute.

Suddenly he sat up, jumped off his bed, and ran downstairs.

"Mom!" he yelled. "I have the
best idea for my science experiment!"

"Finally!" his mom said with
a smile.

After dinner, Max and his mom researched together.

They found lots of cool science experiments about dogs. Max was so excited!

"That one!" cried Max. "That is the best one. It will prove that Buddy understands me."

Max grabbed the phone and called Zoe.

"I'm going to test how Buddy

reads people's faces!" he said.

"What are you talking about?"

asked Zoe.

"For my science experiment,"

said Max.

"Cool!" said Zoe. "But you'll need to test other dogs, too, right?"

"Oh," said Max. "Good idea."

"I know lots of families with dogs," said Zoe. "I can help you."

"Thanks!" Max said.

He hung up the phone and looked up more information on dog behavior.

At last, Max began to write in his science fair journal. Once he started writing, he couldn't stop.

Max knew he had the perfect experiment. He  couldn't wait to test all the dogs!

"Dogs and science, my two favorite things," Max said.

That Saturday, Max and Zoe

rounded up seven dogs from friends.

Max got the dogs settled with

some treats. Then the experiment

began!

Zoe took her place on one end of the couch. Max hid on the other side of the couch.

"Buddy first," he whispered to his mom.

She brought Buddy into the living room.

Buddy stared at Zoe. Zoe stared at Buddy. Then Zoe frowned and looked mad. Buddy ran to the kitchen.

Max took notes the whole time.

Then Mom brought Buddy back into the living room.

Zoe stared at him again. Buddy stared back. Then Zoe smiled widely at him. Buddy ran to Zoe and jumped on her lap.

Max and Zoe followed the same procedure with all of the dogs.

Each time, Max watched closely. He took careful notes and recorded the dog's reactions.

"Wow," he thought. "Most of these dogs do understand people!"

On Monday night, Max was ready. So was Buddy.

Max told the crowd, "Dogs can read people's faces, eyes, and hand signs. Watch Buddy read my face."

Max stared at Buddy for a few seconds then frowned.

Buddy covered his head.

Everyone clapped.

"Thank you," Max said.

"Woof!" Buddy barked.

"Dogs really are a boy's best friend," Max said as he hugged Buddy.

"Woof! Woof!" Buddy barked in agreement.

## About the Author

Shelley Swanson Sateren is the award-winning author of many children's books. She has worked as a children's book editor and in a children's bookstore. Today, besides writing, Shelley works with elementary-school-aged children in various settings. She lives in St. Paul, Minnesota, with her husband and two sons.

## About the Illustrator

Mary Sullivan has been drawing and writing her whole life, which has mostly been spent in Texas. She earned her BFA from the University of Texas in Studio Art, but she considers herself a self-trained illustrator. Mary lives in Cedar Park, a suburb of Austin, Texas.

# Glossary

**behavior (bi-HAYV-yuhr)** — the way someone acts

**experiment (ek-SPER-uh-ment)** — a scientific test to try out a theory or to see the effect of something

**procedure (pruh-SEE-jur)** — a way of doing something, usually by using a series of steps

**reaction (ree-AK-shuhn)** — a response to an action

**research (REE-surch)** — to study and find out about a subject

**topic (TOP-ik)** — the subject of a discussion, study, lesson, speech, or piece of writing

# Discussion Questions

1. Max had a hard time picking a topic for his science experiment. If you did a science experiment, what topic would you pick? Why?

2. Do you think it's a good idea to use an animal for a science experiment? Why or why not?

3. Were you surprised with the results of Max's experiment? Why or why not?

# Writing Prompts

1. What is the best thing you ever did in science class? Write down your answer and reason.

2. Make a list of three commands that many dogs understand. Then add one more command that you wish a dog could understand.

3. Zoe helped Max with his science experiment. Write about a time when you helped a friend.

# Make Your Own Dog Treats

Just like kids, dogs enjoy a good treat. Make your own dog treats for that special dog in your life.

**Tools:**

- oven mitts
- knife
- cutting board
- measuring cups
- teaspoon
- large mixing bowl
- small mixing bowl
- big mixing spoon
- 2 baking sheets (ungreased)
- 1 drinking glass
- spatula

**Ingredients:**

- 1 big apple
- 1/4 cup honey
- 1/2 cup water
- 1 cup oatmeal
- 1/2 teaspoon cinnamon
- 1 1/2 cups whole wheat flour
- 1/4 cup white flour

## What you do:

1. Heat the oven to 350 degrees.

2. Have an adult core the apple and cut it into small pieces.

3. In the big bowl, stir together the apple bits, honey, water, oatmeal, and cinnamon. Then stir in the whole wheat flour to make dough.

4. Fill the teaspoon with a spoonful of dough. Cover the baking sheets with spoonfuls of dough, two inches apart.

5. Put the white flour into the small bowl. Dip the bottom of the glass into the flour. Press the bottom of the glass onto each ball of dough to make the cookies flat.

6. Bake the cookies for 30 minutes. Ask an adult to take the cookies out of the oven and flip them over with the spatula.

7. Turn the oven to 325 degrees. Bake the cookies for 30 more minutes.

8. Let the cookies cool, and then let your dog have a treat.

# The Fun Doesn't Stop Here!

Discover more at www.capstonekids.com

- Videos & Contests
- Games & Puzzles
- Friends & Favorites
- Authors & Illustrators

Find cool websites and more books like this one at www.facthound.com. Just type in the Book ID 9781404872028 and you're ready to go!